LITTLE CRITTER'S FAMILY TREASURY

Written and illustrated by Mercer Mayer

Random House  New York

Random House 🏠 New York

Little Critter's Family Treasury book, characters, text, and images copyright © 2018 by Mercer Mayer.

Little Critter, Mercer Mayer's Little Critter, and Mercer Mayer's Little Critter and Logo are registered trademarks of Orchard House Licensing Company.

All rights reserved. Published in the United States by Random House Children's Books, a division of Penguin Random House LLC, New York, and in Canada by Penguin Random House Canada Limited, Toronto. The stories in this collection were originally published separately in the United States by Golden Books, an imprint of Random House Children's Books, New York, in 1977, 1983, 1985, 1990, and 1991.

Random House and the colophon are registered trademarks of Penguin Random House LLC.

Visit us on the Web!
rhcbooks.com
littlecritter.com
ISBN 978-1-5247-6619-1
MANUFACTURED IN CHINA
10 9 8 7 6 5 4 3 2 1

CONTENTS

Just Me and My Mom

Just Me and My Dad

Just Me and My Little Brother

Me Too!

Just Grandma and Me

Just Grandpa and Me

Just Me and My Puppy

JUST ME AND MY MOM

BY
MERCER MAYER

We went to the city,
just me and my mom.
Mom gave me some money
to buy tickets for the train.

I wanted to help Mom get on the train
but the steps were too high.
So Mom helped me instead.

But when the conductor came by,
the tickets were gone.
So Mom paid the conductor
some more money.

The city was very busy.
I held Mom's hand so she
wouldn't be scared.

We went to the Museum
of Natural History.
They had rooms full of
old dinosaur bones.

I picked up a little dinosaur egg
to show my mom.
But someone ran up and grabbed it.
I wasn't going to hurt it.

I tried on some costumes,
just for Mom.
But the museum guard
didn't like that.

Then we went next door
to the Aquarium.

There were lots of fish
in a big tank of water.

They had some seals doing a show.
Mom got mad because
she couldn't find me.
I ran up front to get
a closer look at the seals.

We went to the art museum,
but it only had a lot of weird pictures
and I was getting tired.

After that, we went to a very
nice restaurant for lunch.
We didn't stay, though.

We decided to have a hot dog from
a stand. That was more fun anyway.

Mom wanted to go to a big store
full of dresses and stuff like that. Yuck.

Mom even made me try on some clothes.
She bought me a new suit.
Some guy measured me and stuck pins all over
my clothes.

We passed by the toys.
I found the stuffed animal
I always wanted
but Mom said, "It's time to go."

We took a taxi to the train station.
I got to ride in the front seat.
The taxi driver drove real fast.
That was cool.

I let Mom buy the tickets this time.
She said she didn't have
enough money to buy more tickets
if these got lost.
"Good idea, Mom!"

We had fun, just me and my mom.
I even stayed awake
all the way home—well, almost.

JUST ME AND MY DAD

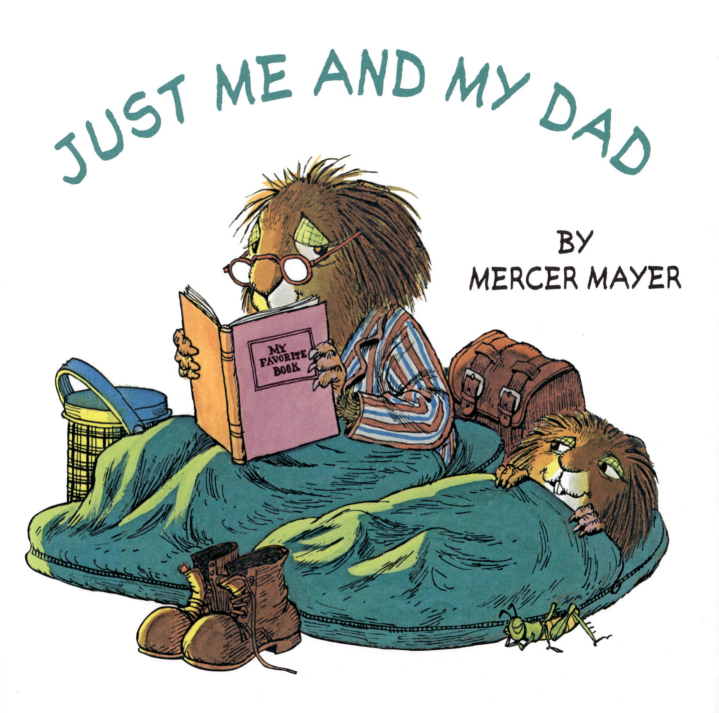

BY
MERCER MAYER

MY FAVORITE BOOK.

We went camping,
just me and my dad.
Dad drove the car
because I'm too little.

I picked the campsite, but someone
was already living there.
So I gave it back.

We found another
campsite nearby.
My dad was tired,
so I pitched the tent.

We made a campfire.
I found the wood,
and my dad lit the fire.

I wanted to take my dad
for a ride in our canoe,
but I launched it too hard.

We went fishing instead.

My dad took a snapshot
of the fish we caught.
Then I cooked dinner
for me and my dad.

We had eggs.

After dinner, I told my dad a ghost story.
Boy, did he get scared!

I gave my dad a big hug.
That made him feel better.

Then we went to bed.

I stayed up with my dad and let him read a story to me.

We slept in our tent all night long—
just me and my dad.

JUST ME AND MY LITTLE BROTHER

BY
MERCER MAYER

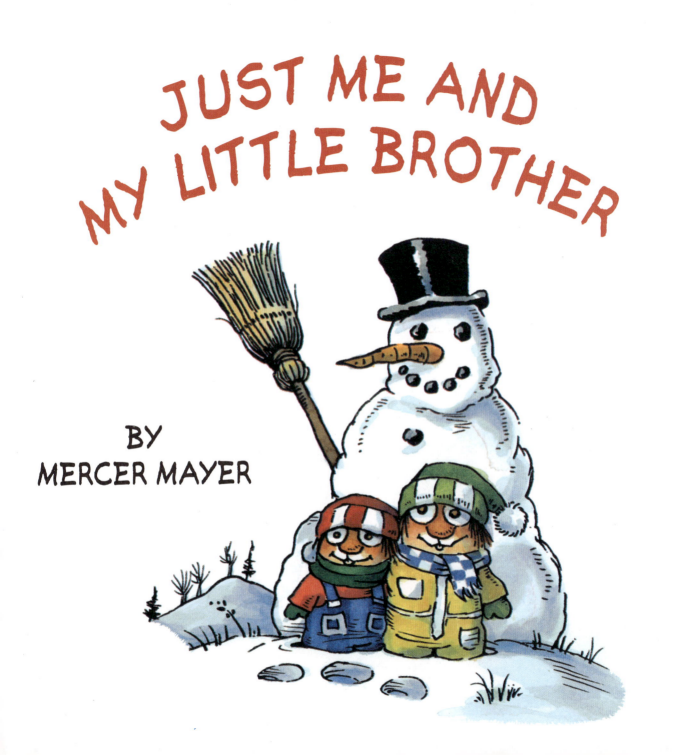

We will do everything together,
just me and my little brother.
We will go to the orchard to pick apples,
and I will help him climb up.

We will have bunk beds,
and I will have the top
'cause I'm bigger.

We can play space wars.

We will be real tough,
just me and my little brother.

The bully will run away
when we come around.

We will stay up late and watch
the spooky shows on TV,
just me and my little brother.

At birthday parties we will eat
the most ice cream and cake,
just me and my little brother.

We can play cowboys and Indians,
and I'll let him catch me.

On Halloween we can go
trick-or-treating together,
just me and my little brother.

At Thanksgiving we will break
the wishbone, and I will let him win.

In the winter we will build a snowman.

We will build a snow fort
and have snowball fights.
Just me and my little brother
will be on the same side.

On Christmas morning
we will share our presents.

At Easter time we will hunt eggs together,
just me and my little brother.
And if he finds the most eggs,
I won't mind.

I will teach my little brother
to ride his bicycle.

He will have to practice a while.

We will play all day
and never get tired.

There are so many
things we can do,
just me and my little brother.

Goo!

But first he'll have to
learn how to walk.

ME TOO!

BY MERCER MAYER

When my little sister saw
me riding my skateboard,
she said . . .

Me too!

Then I had to help her ride.

I had a paper airplane
that I made myself.
But my little sister
saw it and said . . .

Me too!

Then she threw it
in a tree.

I went hiking with my friends and
my little sister said, "Me too!"

I had to carry her because she got tired.

Guess what my little sister said.

I went skating on the pond.
My little sister said, "Me too!"
She doesn't know how to skate,
so I had to hold her up.

Me too!

There was one last piece of cake.
My little sister said . . .

I had to cut it in half,
even though I saw it first.

When I went fishing
she said, "Me too!"
Then she caught
the biggest fish.

I went to my secret tree house. My little sister said . . .

Me too!

Mom said I had to help her up.

Everything I do
my little sister says,
"Me too!"

Today my little sister
had a candy cane of
her very own.

So I said...

Guess what my little sister said.

JUST GRANDMA AND ME

BY MERCER MAYER

We went to the beach,
just Grandma and me.

I wanted to set up the beach umbrella,

but the wind was too strong.

I flew my kite instead.

I bought hot dogs for Grandma and me,
but they fell in the sand.
So I washed them off.

I found a nice seashell for Grandma,
but it was full of a crab.

I wanted to blow up my sea horse,
but I didn't have enough air.
So Grandma helped a little.

I told Grandma to take me
way out in the deep water,

but not too far.

I put on my fins and my mask
and showed Grandma how I can snorkel.

I dug a hole in the sand for Grandma.
Then I covered her up and tickled her toes.

I built a sandcastle just for Grandma, but a big wave came.

Grandma said that's what happens
to sandcastles, and we will build
a new one next time.

On the way home Grandma was tired,
so I told her I would watch for our stop.

We had a good time at the beach,
just Grandma and me.

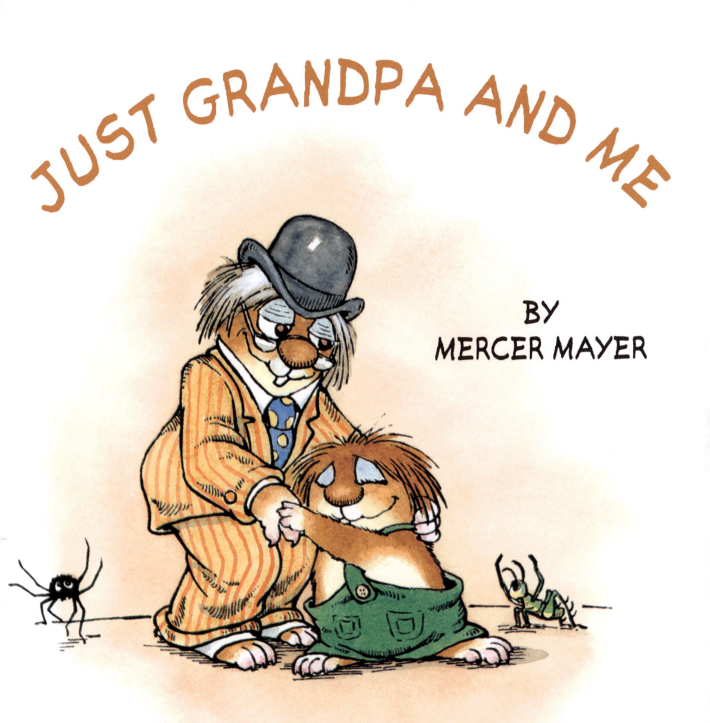

JUST GRANDPA AND ME

BY
MERCER MAYER

My mom said I need a new suit.

So we went to the city to buy one,
just Grandpa and me.

I bought the train tickets,
but I let Grandpa pay.

I taught Grandpa how to sing "Ninety-Nine Bottles of Pop on the Wall."

We went to the big department store.
The revolving door went around and
around and around.

We went around, too,
just Grandpa and me.

I held Grandpa's hand
so he wouldn't get lost.

He did anyway.

Lucky for Grandpa I found him
right away.

CRITTER
SUITS →

We took the escalator to the
suit department.
I told Grandpa to hold on tight
to the rail.

I looked at all the suits
and found just the right one.

TRY ON ROOM ↓

SALE ON CRITTER SHIRTS!

Very CHEAP STUFF

QUICK SALE

Then Grandpa helped me choose
a shirt and tie.

I put on my new suit
and Grandpa said,
"You sure look great!"

Then we went to the movies.
I sat close to Grandpa
in the scary parts
so he wouldn't be afraid.

We had supper in a Chinese restaurant.
I showed Grandpa how to use chopsticks.

Then we got back on the train.
Grandpa took a nap, but not me.
I couldn't wait for Mom
to see my new suit.

We were so proud—
just Grandpa and me.

JUST ME AND MY PUPPY

BY
MERCER MAYER

I wanted a puppy, just for me.
So I traded my baseball mitt for one.

My baby sister liked him
right away.

And, boy, were Mom and Dad surprised!
They said I could keep him if I took
care of him myself.

So I am taking very good care
of my puppy.
I feed him in the morning.

He eats every bite.

Then I put on his leash and
we go for a walk.

I am teaching my puppy
how to heel.

He is learning how to stay . . .

. . . except when he sees a cat.

My puppy knows lots of tricks . . .

how to sit . . .

how to play dead . . .

. . . and how to roll over.

He still needs some practice.

But he already knows how to fetch.

My puppy is a big help around the house.

He's a good guard dog.

He brings in
the paper
for my dad.

And he keeps me company
while I do my homework.

Sometimes my puppy
gets dirty.

Then I give him a bath.

I get him nice and dry
so he won't catch a cold.

Then we get ready for bed . . .

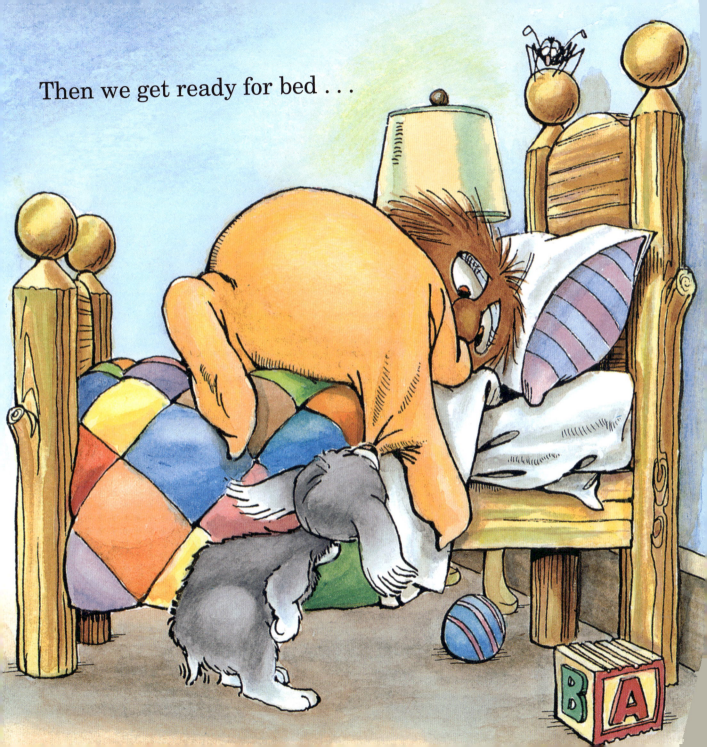

. . . just me and my puppy.